The Old Woman and Her Pig

The story of *The Old Woman and Her Pig* is a British folktale. It is great fun to tell, but in its original form it is decidedly bloodthirsty—"The cat began to kill the rat. The rat began to gnaw the rope. The rope began to hang the butcher. The butcher began to kill the ox . . ." This version isn't intended to replace the original, but rather to provide a lighter alternative.

E.A.K.

To Jessica

E.A.K.

To the two grandmothers of my children,
Miriam and Zipora, and to Grandfather Avraham

G.C.

Text copyright © 1992 by Eric A. Kimmel
Illustrations copyright © 1992 by Giora Carmi
All rights reserved
Printed in the United States of America

Library of Congress Cataloging-in-Publication Data
Kimmel, Eric A.
The old woman and her pig / retold by Eric A. Kimmel ;
illustrated by Giora Carmi.
p.   cm.
Summary: When her newly bought pig won't go over the stile,
an old woman tries to enlist the aid of some reluctant helpers
so that she can get home that night.
ISBN 0-8234-0970-8
[1. Folklore—England.]   I. Carmi, Giora, ill.   II. Title.
PZ8.1.K56701   1992   91-44185   CIP   AC
398.21'0942—dc20
[E]
ISBN 0-8234-1234-2 (pbk.)

The Old Woman
and
Her Pig

adapted by Eric A. Kimmel
illustrated by Giora Carmi

Holiday House / New York

Once upon a time an old woman was sweeping her yard when she found a copper penny. "Today is my lucky day!" the old woman exclaimed. "I will take this penny to market and buy myself a pig."

And that is what she did. She went to the market and bought herself a fine, plump pig. The old woman tied a string around the pig's neck and began leading it home.

They walked and they walked and they walked and they walked, the old woman and her pig, following the road until it came to a wall. Now in the wall was a stile. The pig stopped dead in its tracks, refusing to go another step.

The old woman pulled and she pushed and she pushed and she pulled, but the pig would not go over the stile.

So she looked around and saw a dog. She called to the dog,

"Dog, Dog, nip Pig. Piggy won't go over stile. And I won't get home tonight."

But the dog said, "No!"

o the old woman looked around and saw a stick. She called to the stick,

"Stick, Stick, poke Dog. Dog won't nip Pig. Piggy won't go over stile. And I won't get home tonight."

But the stick said, "No!"

So the old woman looked around and saw some fire. She called to the fire,

"Fire, Fire, burn Stick. Stick won't poke Dog. Dog won't nip Pig. Piggy won't go over stile. And I won't get home tonight."

But the fire said, "No!"

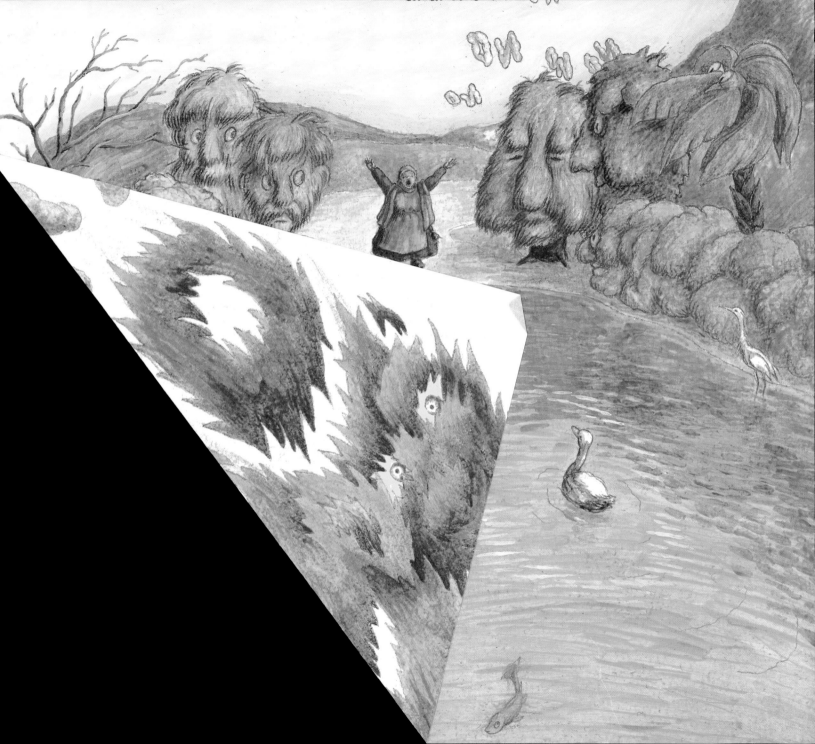

o the old woman looked around and saw some water. She called to the water,

"Water, Water, quench Fire. Fire won't burn Stick. Stick won't poke Dog. Dog won't nip Pig. Piggy won't go over stile. And I won't get home tonight."

But the water said, "No!"

o the old woman looked around and saw a horse. She called to the horse,

"Horse, Horse, drink Water. Water won't quench Fire. Fire won't burn Stick. Stick won't poke Dog. Dog won't nip Pig. Piggy won't go over stile. And I won't get home tonight."

But the horse said, "No!"

So the old woman looked around and saw a rider. She called to the rider,

"Rider, Rider, spur Horse. Horse won't drink Water. Water won't quench Fire. Fire won't burn Stick. Stick won't poke Dog. Dog won't nip Pig. Piggy won't go over stile. And I won't get home tonight."

But the rider said, "No!"

o the old woman looked around and saw a rope. She called to the rope,

"Rope, Rope, lasso Rider. Rider won't spur Horse. Horse won't drink Water. Water won't quench Fire. Fire won't burn Stick. Stick won't poke Dog. Dog won't nip Pig. Piggy won't go over stile. And I won't get home tonight."

But the rope said, "No!"

So the old woman looked around and saw a rat. She called to the rat,

"Rat, Rat, gnaw Rope. Rope won't lasso Rider. Rider won't spur Horse. Horse won't drink Water. Water won't quench Fire. Fire won't burn Stick. Stick won't poke Dog. Dog won't nip Pig. Piggy won't go over stile. And I won't get home tonight."

But the rat said, "No!"

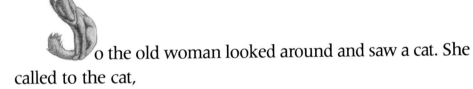

So the old woman looked around and saw a cat. She called to the cat,

"Cat, Cat, chase Rat. Rat won't gnaw Rope. Rope won't lasso Rider. Rider won't spur Horse. Horse won't drink Water. Water won't quench Fire. Fire won't burn Stick. Stick won't poke Dog. Dog won't nip Pig. Piggy won't go over stile. And I won't get home tonight."

But the cat said, "No! Not unless you bring me a saucer of milk."

So the old woman went to visit the cow. "May I please borrow a saucer of milk?" she asked.

But the cow said, "No! Not unless you bring me a handful of hay."

So the old woman went to visit the haystack. "May I please borrow a handful of hay?" she asked.

The haystack did not answer.

The old woman asked again, "May I please borrow a handful of hay?"

The haystack still did not answer.

So the old woman said, "If I may not borrow a handful of hay, please say so."

The haystack did not say anything, which meant that it was all right.

So the old woman borrowed a handful of hay to bring to the cow. The cow was so pleased, she gave the old woman a saucer of milk to bring to the cat. The cat was so pleased, she purred and purred and lapped up all the milk, down to the last drop.

And as soon as the cat finished lapping up the milk . . .

The cat began to chase the rat.
The rat began to gnaw the rope.
The rope began to lasso the rider.
The rider began to spur the horse.
The horse began to drink the water.
The water began to quench the fire.
The fire began to burn the stick.
The stick began to poke the dog.
The dog began to nip the pig.
The piggy jumped over the stile.

nd did the old woman get home that night?

You bet she did!